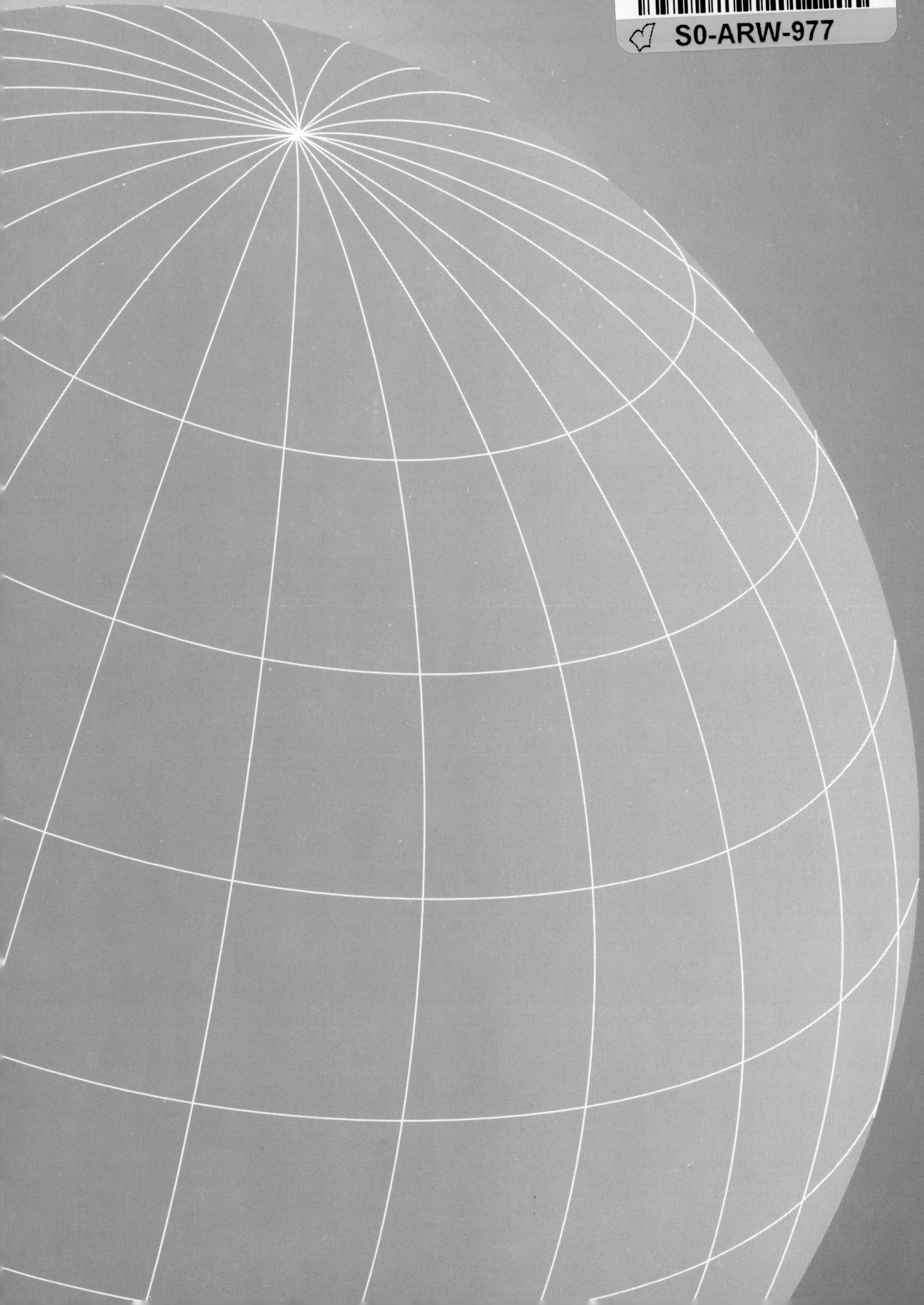

The Little Brown Jay

A Tale from India

Retold by Elizabeth Claire
Illustrated by Miriam Katin
Folklore Consultant: Bette Bosma

MONDO Publishing
One Plaza Road
Greenvale, New York 11548

Copyright © 1994, 1992 by Mondo Publishing
EXPANDED EDITION 1994

Printed in the United States of America
94 95 96 97 98 99   9 8 7 6 5 4 3 2 1

Photograph Credits Scala/Art Resource, NY, Courtesy the Trustees of the British Museum: p. 17; Craig Lovell/Viesti Associates: p. 18; Photo Shot/Bavaria/Viesti Associates: p. 19; Will and Deni McIntyre/Photo Researchers: p. 20; Dilip Mehta/Woodfin Camp & Associates: p. 21 top; S. Nagendra/Photo Researchers: p. 21 bottom.

Library of Congress Cataloging-in-Publication Data
Claire, Elizabeth.
    The little brown jay : a tale from India / retold by Elizabeth Claire ; illustrated by Miriam Katin.
        p. cm.
    Summary: A retelling of a traditional Indian tale in which a little bird helps the beautiful princess Maya through a selfless act of love.
      ISBN 1-879531-17-8 : $21.95. — ISBN 1-879531-44-5 : $9.95. — ISBN 1-879531-23-2 : $4.95
      [1. Folklore—India. 2. Birds—Folklore.] I. Katin, Miriam, ill. II. Title.
III. Series.
PZ8.1.C49   1994
398.24'528—dc20
[E]
                                                94-14366
                                                  CIP
                                                    AC

In India I grew up in a large family, and everyone loved to tell me stories. "And then what happened?" I would ask, and a passing grownup would complete the story someone had begun the night before. The tales were full of wonderful explanations of why animals have their special shapes, colors, and habits. Discover for yourself what happens to the little brown jay.

Veena Oldenburg

Once there was a princess named Maya. She was as beautiful and good as the morning sunshine, but her voice was ugly and sharp.

Every day, handsome young Prince Rama rode by Maya's window. Prince Rama never looked at the beautiful princess. He was blind.

"What can I do?" wondered Maya. She was afraid to speak to him in her ugly voice. Rama did not know she was there.

One day, Maya heard a little jay singing in her garden. The jay was a plain brown bird, but its voice was the sweetest in all of India.

Maya began to cry. The jay
stopped singing. "Beautiful lady,
why are you crying?"

"Beauty is nothing to me," said
Maya. "I wish I could sing like you."

"Please don't cry," said the little brown jay. "I will give you my voice."

"But how?" asked Princess Maya.

"At midnight, tonight, go to the lotus pool," said the jay. "Pick the largest lotus flower. Hold it and make your wish."

That night,
the moon was full, and the air
was cold. Maya put on her
beautiful blue silk scarf and
went down to the lotus pool.

She picked the largest lotus flower in the pool and made her wish: "I wish I had a voice like the little brown jay's."

The magic worked.
Maya began to sing
the sweetest sounds
she had ever heard.
"My wish has come true!"
she cried in her beautiful
new voice.

"I'm glad I could help you," said a sharp voice beside her. It was the little brown jay.

"Oh, thank you! Thank you!" said Maya.

She looked at the jay. "You poor thing, you are shivering from the cold. Let me put my scarf around you."

"I'm warm now," said the jay in his sharp new voice. "And this color is lovely."

"Yes," said Maya. "I wish you could always wear blue."

Instantly, the jay's feathers took the color of the scarf. "Oh thank you, Princess!"

"Don't thank me," Maya said. "It was the magic lotus flower."

The next day, Prince Rama heard Maya singing. They fell in love and were very happy. Even happier was a beautiful new bird— the little blue jay.

In every part of the world people tell pourquoi (*pur-kwa*), or why, stories to explain why things are the way they are. The story of Princess Maya and the little brown jay is one of these tales from India.

Traditional painting of Indian princess.

Palace gate with towers and pillars.

Pourquoi tales are told in many places. From many South American countries come stories that tell how the sun gave animals their different colors. A tale from Norway answers the question, "Why do bears have stumpy tales?" A Ngoni pourquoi story from Africa tells why monkeys live in trees. And an Aboriginal tale from Australia explains why some birds make their special sounds.

In *The Little Brown Jay*, the pictures show how princesses and princes in India lived more than 300 years ago. Maya lives in a big white palace with tall towers and pillars. Everything is beautifully decorated, even Rama's horse. And the artist decorated the pages with borders showing repeated pictures of objects from the story, such as the magic lotus flower.

Lotus flowers.

India today is a mixture of old and new. In cities, old palaces and temples stand next to modern buildings. Some men wear traditional loose-fitting clothes, and some women wear saris, fabric draped like dresses. Others wear clothes like people in North America.

India's big cities are large and crowded. The streets are full of bicycles, carts, and cars. Some people live in apartments, while others live in small houses

City people wearing traditional and modern clothing.

**Painted elephants
at a festival.**

just outside town. City
children go to school,
but in many villages
children stay home
and work with their
families.

The people's love of beauty can be seen in their
paintings, clothing, and jewelry. Even the
elephants people ride at festivals are painted with
designs. In villages,
local artists paint
stories on paper, and
people gather to
listen to the artists
tell their stories.

**Artist painting
a story picture.**

21

INSIDE
TANKS
AND HEAVY
ARTILLERY

The crew of a Paladin, an
American self-propelled gun

Thanks to the creative team:
Senior Editor: Alice Peebles
Fact Checking: Tom Jackson
Illustrations: Martin Bustamante
Picture Research: Nic Dean
Design: www.collaborate.agency

Hungry Tomato®
A division of Lerner Publishing Group, Inc.
241 First Avenue North
Minneapolis, MN 55401 USA

For reading levels and more information, look up
this title at www.lernerbooks.com.

Main body text set in Avenir Next Condensed Medium 11/15.
Typeface provided by Linotype AG.

Library of Congress Cataloging-in-Publication Data

Names: Oxlade, Chris, author.
Title: Inside tanks and heavy artillery / Chris Oxlade.
Description: Minneapolis : Hungry Tomato, [2018] | Series: Inside
military machines | Includes index. | Audience: Grades 4-6. |
Audience: Ages 8-12.
Identifiers: LCCN 2017014444 (print) | LCCN 2017012915
(ebook) | ISBN 9781512450019 (eb pdf) |
ISBN 9781512432268 (lb : alk. paper)
Subjects: LCSH: Tanks (Military science)–Juvenile literature. |
Artillery–Juvenile literature.
Classification: LCC UG446.5 (print) | LCC UG446.5 .O947 2018
(ebook) | DDC 623.4/1–dc23

LC record available at https://lccn.loc.gov/2017014444

Manufactured in the United States of America
1-41781-23542-4/4/2017

INSIDE
TANKS AND
HEAVY ARTILLERY

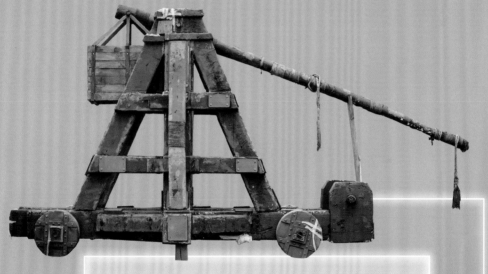

The twelfth-century trebuchet worked like a seesaw. A huge weight at one end dropped, making the arm rise to throw a stone ball high into the air.

by Chris Oxlade

HUNGRY TOMATO®

Minneapolis

A British Challenger 2 main battle tank, one of the world's most advanced battle machines

Contents

BATTLE MACHINES: TANKS AND ARTILLERY

Modern tanks, with their big guns and thick armor, are complex battle machines, filled with the latest technology. They are devastating weapons in battle that punch holes in enemy defensive formations. Modern artillery is similarly high-tech. An artillery piece is a big gun. It delivers an **explosive shell** with great accuracy, often at a **range** of many miles. These amazing weapons are the result of a long history of development that began thousands of years ago.

British Mark I

Length: 26 feet (8 meters)

Width: 13 feet (4 m)

Weight: 31 tons (28 metric tons)

Engine: 3-gallon (13 liters) gasoline

Top speed: 4 miles (6 kilometers) per hour

Weapons: two 6-pound guns / three machine guns

Armor: 0.2- to 0.5-inch (6- to 12-millimeter) steel

Crew: 8

British Mark I Tank

This was the first successful tank, introduced in 1916 to the battlefields of World War I (1914–1918). It had a gun in each side turret, machine guns, and metal armor. But the tank was unreliable and easily damaged.

Old and New

The two machines here show how the technology of tanks has changed over the last one hundred years. Below left is a tank that fought in World War I, the first war where tanks played an important part. Below right is a large modern tank, full of technology that makes it deadly in a fight.

M1A1 Abrams

Length: 26 feet (8 m)

Width: 13 feet (4 m)

Weight: 63 tons (57 metric tons)

Engine: gas turbine

Top speed: 45 miles (72 km) per hour

Weapons: 120 mm gun / three machine guns

Armor: 24-inch (600 mm) composite

Crew: 4

M1A1 Abrams

This is a modern tank operated by the United States Army and other armies around the world. It features a powerful gun on a rotating turret that fires explosive shells, computerized gun aiming, and armor made from advanced materials.

ANCIENT WEAPONS

Early artillery weapons were invented thousands of years ago. They were mechanical, using giant levers or springs to fire rocks, huge arrows, and even dead animals at the enemy. There were also armored machines on wheels. Many ancient weapons were designed for **siege** warfare: attackers tried to break down walls with heavy **projectiles** and battering rams, and fired projectiles over the walls to target the defenders.

An Ancient Arsenal

Here is a selection of ancient weapons used for attacking troops and fortifications. These were all in use about 2,500 years ago. Some similar weapons were reinvented in medieval times, but often they were not as good as the Roman versions.

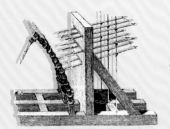

Arrow launcher: This machine fired a hail of arrows at once.

Mounted crossbow: This was a giant crossbow on a stand that was aimed by hand.

Siege tower: This tower was rolled up to walls to allow attackers to storm inside.

Suspended battering ram: This type of battering ram was rocked backward and forward to ram walls.

Sliding battering ram: This battering ram was operated by pulling ropes, making it slide forward and backward.

Ballista: This Roman machine was like a giant crossbow that fired spears more than 2,000 feet (600 m).

Onagar: This machine used a tightly twisted rope as a spring to throw projectiles.

Siege Warfare

During a siege, attackers often built tall, armored towers on wheels, called siege towers or siege engines. They pushed the towers up against defensive walls, allowing soldiers to reach their attackers. This painting shows the siege engines at the siege of Constantinople (modern-day Instanbul) in 1453. By this time, early **cannons** were in use too.

EARLY CANNONS

In late medieval times, a single innovation changed the world of weapons for good. That was the use of **gunpowder** in artillery, which would continue for hundreds of years. Gunpowder is a mixture of saltpeter, charcoal, and sulphur, which burns very fast, creating a flash, a bang, and lots of hot gas. Inventors realized that the gas could propel a stone or metal ball from a metal tube, making the first simple cannons possible.

Chinese Fire Arrows

Gunpowder, or black powder, was probably invented in China in the ninth century CE, before its use spread to the rest of the world. The Chinese used it to launch rockets—known as fire arrows—at their enemies. They may have used the powder in simple cannons too.

Pot-de-fer

This fourteenth-century weapon's name means "iron pot." It was like an iron vase lying on its side, about 3 feet (1 m) long, with a small hole leading into the center. Gunpowder was poured into the pot, then an arrow-like projectile was inserted. The arrow was wrapped in leather so it would fit tightly. Lighting the gunpowder through a touch hole shot the arrow away.

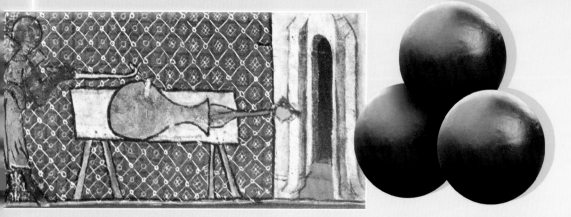

The Siege of Orleans

This 1428 painting of a famous French siege shows a typical late-medieval cannon. The cannon was made of lengths of **wrought iron** held together by iron hoops for strength. Later in the fifteenth century, cannon-makers began to **cast** bronze cannons, which were lighter and stronger than iron cannons. They remained the main type of cannon for around four hundred years.

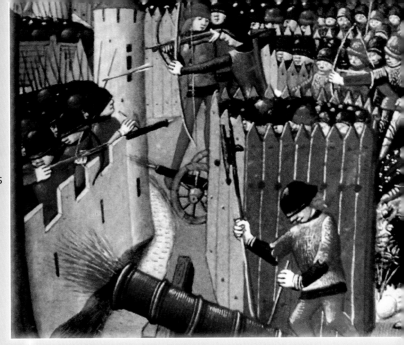

Bombard

Armies besieging castles and cities used massive cannons called bombards. They fired enormous stone balls that smashed defensive walls to bits. However, they were very hard to move around. This huge bronze bombard, now on display in Moscow, Russia, is called the Tsar Cannon. It was made in 1586 and was probably never fired.

IMPROVING ARTILLERY

The artillery of the early nineteenth century was not much different from the cannons of three centuries before. But from the mid-nineteenth century, huge technical advances meant that artillery became more powerful, more destructive, and more accurate. Explosive shells replaced solid **cannonballs**, powerful explosives replaced gunpowder, and artillery pieces became easier to load.

Rodman 20-inch Gun

Shown left is one of the largest guns of the American Civil War (1861–1865). Thomas Rodman, a Union artillery expert, designed it. He invented a way of casting that made the barrel much stronger than ever before. The gun had a very large **bore** and could fire a 0.33-ton (0.3 metric ton) projectile more than 4 miles (7 km).

Artillery in Action

By the American Civil War, some guns had **rifling**, spiral grooves that made shells spin as they moved through the barrel. Rifling made shells fly much straighter than they had from older guns.

Siege Mortar

In a **mortar**, the barrel is quite short compared to its diameter. Its job is to throw a very heavy explosive charge high into the air, so that the charge lands almost vertically. This mortar, nicknamed The Dictator, saw action at the Siege of Petersburg during the American Civil War, where it destroyed Confederate gun positions.

The Dictator

Barrel length: 53 inches (135 centimeters)

Bore diameter: 13 inches (33 cm)

Weight: 9 tons (8 metric tons)

Projectile: 220-pound mortar shell

Range: 2.5 miles (4 km)

Date: 1862

The Shell

A shell is a hollow projectile, filled with explosive materials. Simple gunpowder-filled shells were in use by the sixteenth century. In 1784, British artillery officer Henry Shrapnel invented a shell filled with bullets and an explosive charge. The charge blew the shell apart in midair, releasing a deadly shower of bullets. All modern shells are round with a pointed end. The shell shown here was developed in the mid-nineteenth century.

THE FIRST ARMORED VEHICLES

The idea of an armored battle vehicle is thousands of years old. In ancient times, warriors went into battle on chariots, and the siege tower could be thought of as a simple armored vehicle. True armored vehicles became possible with the development of mechanical power, such as the steam engine and the internal combustion engine in the nineteenth century.

Chariots

Warriors first charged into battle on chariots more than 4,000 years ago. These fast, two-wheeled carts had a shield at the front, and the warrior was armed with a bow and arrow, spears, and swords. This mosaic shows Alexander the Great fighting from a chariot.

Leonardo da Vinci's Tank

A sketch drawn in about 1485 by the famous Italian artist and engineer Leonardo da Vinci shows an armored vehicle armed with small guns. This model was made from studying the sketch, but the vehicle was never actually made. The sketch shows that the machine would have been moved by hand cranks inside.

Model-T Fighting Car

Early mechanized gun carriers, such as this 1913 British Model-T MG, were cars with machine guns added to them. Hundreds of these were used as armed patrol cars in desert warfare in World War I.

Simms Motor War Car

Length: 28 feet (8.5 m)

Width: 7 feet (2 m)

Armor: 0.2-inch (6 mm) steel

Weapons: two Maxim machine guns

Engine: 0.8-gallon (3 L) gasoline

Crew: 4

Simms Motor War Car

This extraordinary British machine was the first fully armored fighting vehicle and was completed in 1902. The designer and builder was Frederick Simms. Simms started with a frame and engine from a large car, and added a body of 0.2-inch (6 mm) armor, with pointed ends for ramming. The machine was never used in battle.

BIG GUNS

Artillery played an enormous part in World War I. Armies dug hundreds of miles of defensive trenches and attacked each other with huge artillery barrages, which often lasted for many hours. Most of the time the enemy was far away and out of sight, but gunners used information from spotters to figure out which way to aim their guns.

World War I Artillery

These Belgian gunners set up their **field artillery** on the Western Front during World War I. The gun has a metal shield to protect the crew from gunfire and **shrapnel**. The positions of enemy guns were found by observing their sounds and flashes from different positions on the front line.

Ammunition Supplies

The big guns of World War I needed a constant supply of shells. These were made in giant ammunition factories such as this one in Britain. As well as high-explosive shells, there were shells for producing smoke across the battlefield, and incendiary shells that spread fire.

Monster Guns

During World War II (1939–1945), the Germans built enormous guns for launching massive high-explosive shells at targets dozens of miles way. The gun pictured, named Dora, was the biggest of the war. It fired shells 31.5 inches (80 centimeters) in diameter and weighed nearly 5.5 tons (5 metric tons)! The shells could go through 23 feet (7 m) of concrete, or 3 feet (1 m) of solid steel. Dora was mounted on railroad cars that moved along two parallel railroad tracks.

Big Gun in Action

Dora was ready for action in the Soviet Union (a nation that existed from 1922 to 1991, based in modern-day Russia) but was never used. Another similar gun, called Heavy Gustav, was used when Germany invaded the Soviet Union in 1941–1942, to attack the city of Sevastopol in Crimea.

Dora

Length: 154 feet (47 m)

Width: 23 feet (7 m)

Barrel length: 108 feet (33 m)

Bore diameter: 31.5 inches (80 cm)

Range: 24 miles (39 km)

Weight: 1,488 tons
(1,350 metric tons)

THE FIRST TANKS

Before World War I began, the military authorities in most countries didn't think tanks would be useful on the battlefield as they were used to fighting with foot soldiers and horses. But World War I became a trench war, with armies facing each other across battlefields covered in holes from exploded shells. Generals soon realized that an armored vehicle that could move across the rough, muddy ground would be useful for attacking enemy positions.

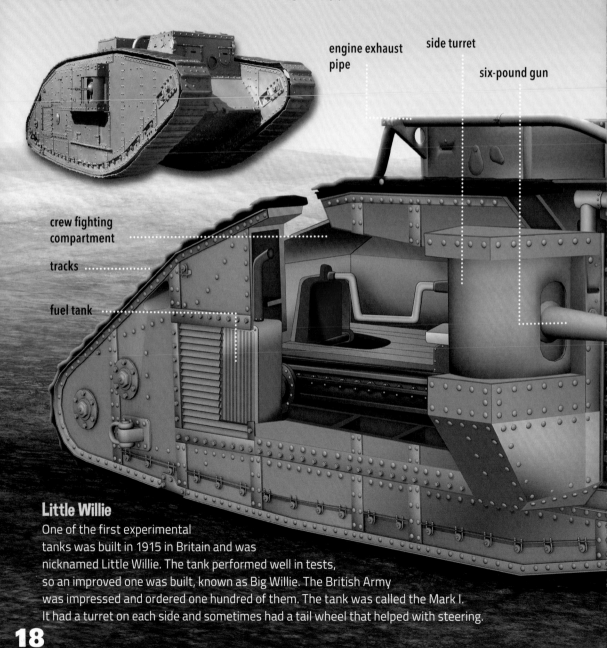

engine exhaust pipe

side turret

six-pound gun

crew fighting compartment

tracks

fuel tank

Little Willie

One of the first experimental tanks was built in 1915 in Britain and was nicknamed Little Willie. The tank performed well in tests, so an improved one was built, known as Big Willie. The British Army was impressed and ordered one hundred of them. The tank was called the Mark I. It had a turret on each side and sometimes had a tail wheel that helped with steering.

The Battle of Cambrai

The Mark I tank was slow, the tracks often broke, and the engine often stalled. In 1917, however, 474 much-improved Mark IV tanks took part in the Battle of Cambrai. They broke through the German lines. The battle showed that tanks had come of age.

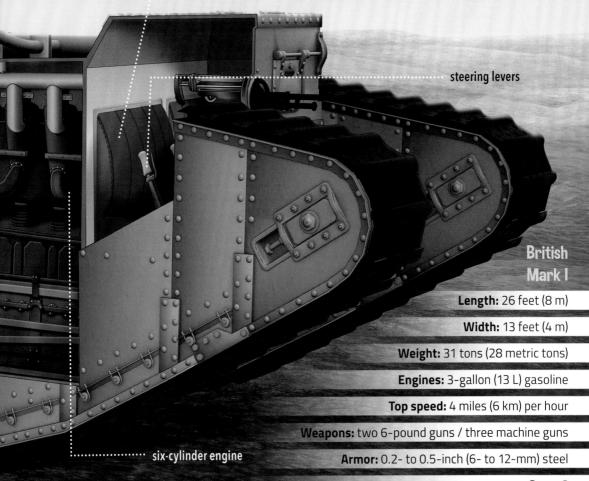

driver's cab

steering levers

six-cylinder engine

British Mark I

Length:	26 feet (8 m)
Width:	13 feet (4 m)
Weight:	31 tons (28 metric tons)
Engines:	3-gallon (13 L) gasoline
Top speed:	4 miles (6 km) per hour
Weapons:	two 6-pound guns / three machine guns
Armor:	0.2- to 0.5-inch (6- to 12-mm) steel
Crew:	8

TANKS OF WORLD WAR II

After World War I, tanks became bigger, faster, and better armed and armored. World War II began with devastating attacks by huge formations of German tanks–the **panzer** divisions. Germany and the Soviet Union built even larger and more powerful tanks as the war continued.

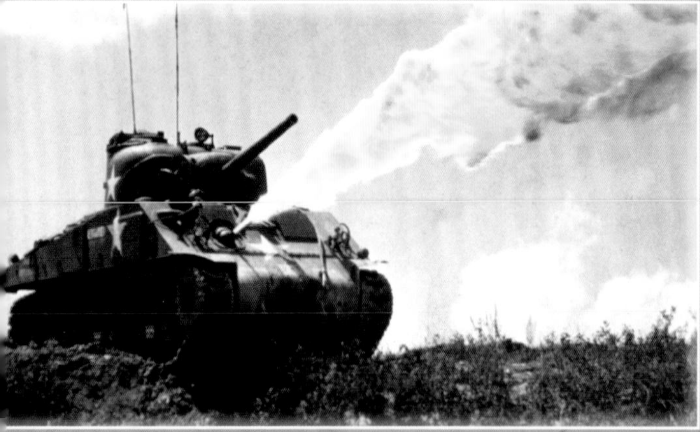

M4 Sherman

The M4 Sherman was the main Allied tank of World War II. The Sherman was built for speed and mobility rather than firepower and armor. In a one-on-one fight it was no match for German Tiger (*below*) and **Panther** tanks, but it was successful while fighting in packs.

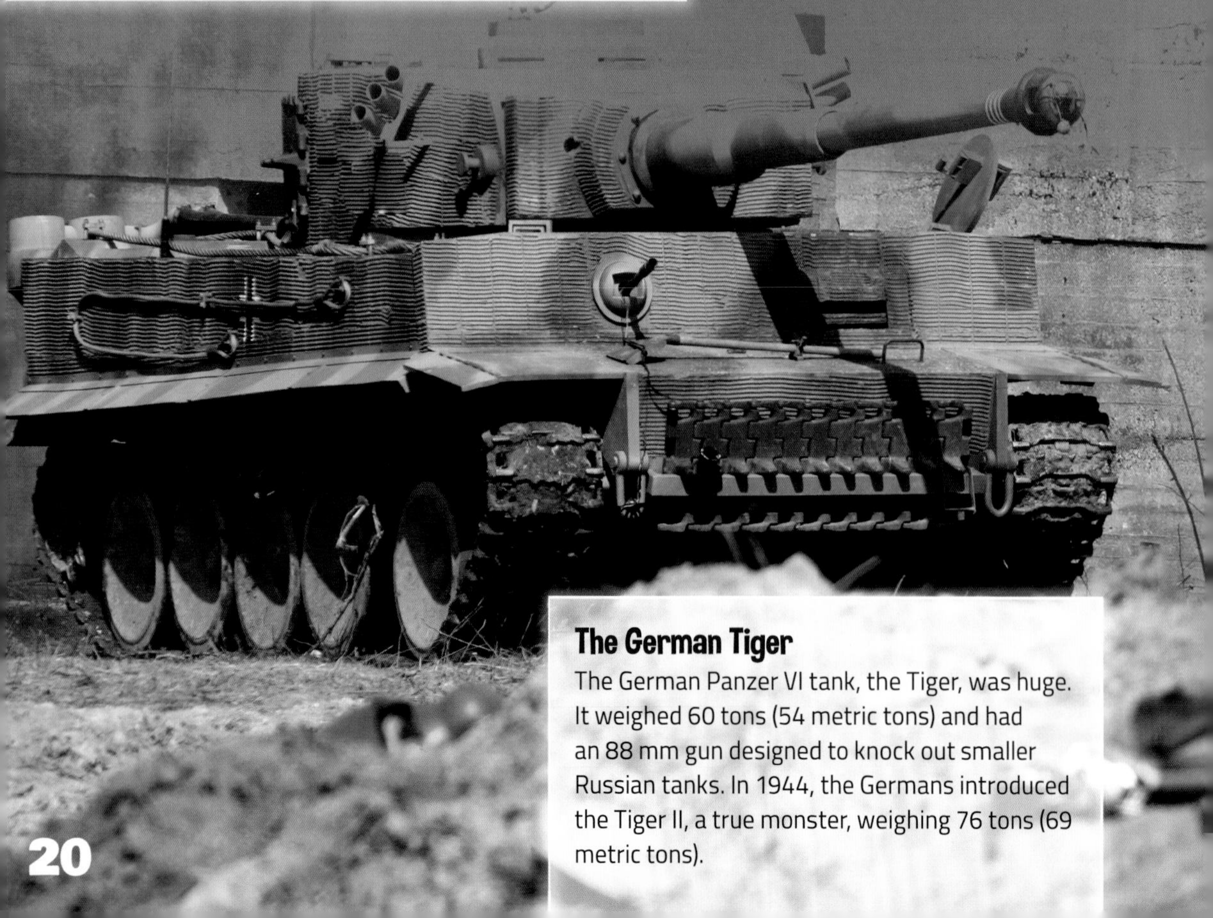

The German Tiger

The German Panzer VI tank, the Tiger, was huge. It weighed 60 tons (54 metric tons) and had an 88 mm gun designed to knock out smaller Russian tanks. In 1944, the Germans introduced the Tiger II, a true monster, weighing 76 tons (69 metric tons).

The Russian T-34

The T-34 was the main Russian tank of World War II. At 31 tons (28 metric tons), it was a medium rather than a heavy tank. But its 76 mm gun could destroy all but the biggest German tanks. Also, its thick armor sloped, making shells bounce off.

Panzer VI Tiger

Length: 20 feet (6 m)

Width: 13 feet (4 m)

Engine: Maybach V-12

Weight: 59.5 tons (54 metric tons)

Top speed: 28 miles (45 km) per hour

Weapons: 88 mm gun / 2 machine guns

Armor: 1- to 5-inch (25- to 120-mm) steel

Crew: 5

Eastern Front Battles

Russian T-34s and German Tigers were some of the tanks that fought on the Eastern Front in 1942–1945. In 1943 the Germans, pushed back by the Russians, made a stand near the Russian city of Kursk. Around 3,000 Germans and around 6,000 Russian tanks were involved in the Battle of Kursk. It was the largest tank battle in history and a victory for the Russians.

MODERN ARTILLERY

Even though tanks carry powerful guns, armies still use artillery pieces to attack enemy positions. All modern artillery is field artillery–it can be moved to where it's needed. There are two types: towed artillery, which is towed from place to place, and **self-propelled artillery**, where the artillery piece is mounted on a vehicle. Artillery can also be moved by helicopter.

Rocket Launchers

Rockets are self-propelled projectiles with rocket engines and an explosive charge. Rocket launchers are often thought of as artillery, although the rockets are self-propelled rather than fired by a gun. This is a Russian Buratino multiple rocket launcher.

Modern Shells

Shells are round with a pointed end. The main type is the high-explosive shell. This is a metal canister containing an explosive charge and a fuse. The fuse sets off the charge when the shell arrives at its target. Other types include the armor-piercing shell, the illuminating shell, which lights up a battlefield, and the smoke shell.

Self-propelled Artillery

A self-propelled artillery piece is a cross between a tank and a gun. Here, inside an American M109 Paladin, the 155 mm gun is ready to fire. The crew is protected from small-arms fire and explosions outside by thin armor.

M198 Howitzer

Barrel length: 20 feet (6 m)

Length: 36 feet (11 m)

Weight: 8 tons (7 metric tons)

Bore Diameter: 6 inches (155 mm)

Maximum range: 14 miles (22 km)

Crew: 9

Field Howitzer

A modern field gun is towed into position by a support truck, which carries the crew, ammunition, and other equipment. In position, the gun's legs are folded out to stabilize it. The gun is aimed by swivelling it from side to side and angling the barrel to adjust the range.

MODERN TANKS

Modern tanks still look very similar to the tanks that fought in World War II—they have an armored body, two tracks, a revolving turret, and a big gun. However, modern tanks have better speed and handling as well as stronger armor, making them safer for their crews. They also have computerized targeting and aiming systems, so their guns are very accurate, even when the tank is moving on rough ground.

Firing the Gun

On top of the tank is a digital sighting system to identify targets such as other tanks. The crew selects one of the targets, and the angles of the turret and the gun are automatically adjusted so the shell will hit the target. Tanks fire armor-piercing shells to knock out enemy tanks. These pierce through armor before exploding.

Challenger 2

The British Challenger 2 tank has a 120 mm gun controlled by a laser rangefinder and a digital fire computer. The Challenger 2 has some of the toughest armor of any modern tank. The hull and turret are protected by Chobham armor, made from a **composite material** made up of ceramics, metals, and plastics.

Crew Protection

The Leopard 2A6 (*right*) is the German army's main battle tank. As in other modern tanks, the crew is protected inside an airtight compartment. In a nuclear, biological, or chemical attack, air is filtered as it goes in. There is also a system for putting out fires instantly.

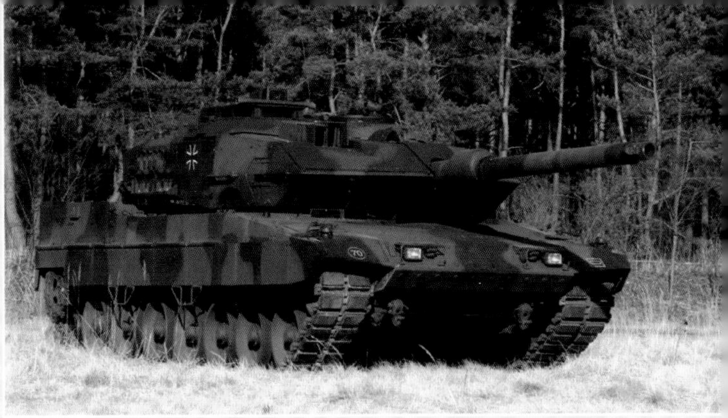

Challenger 2

Length: 26 feet (8 m)

Width: 11.5 feet (3.5 m)

Weight: 69 tons (62.5 metric tons)

Engines: Diesel V-12

Top speed: 37 miles (59 km) per hour

Weapons: 120 mm gun/chain gun/machine gun

Armor: Composite

Crew: 4

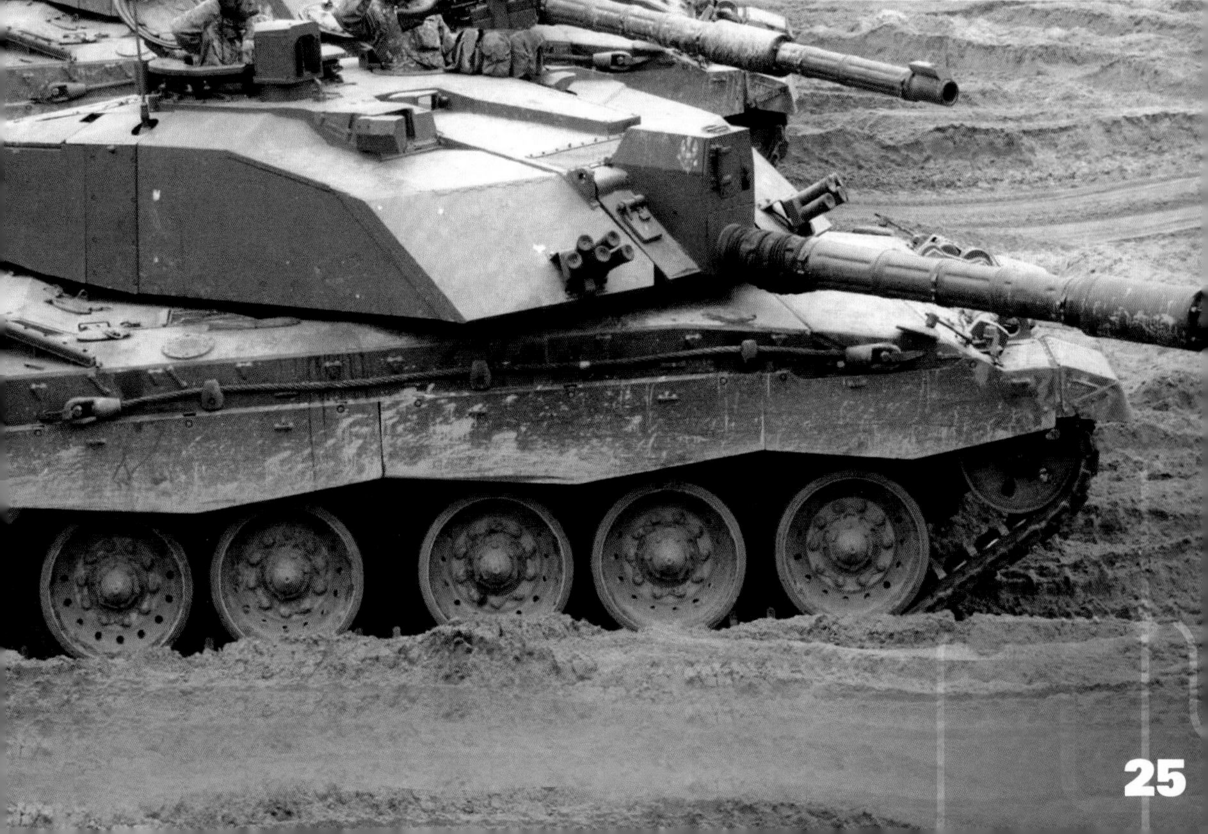

ABRAMS BATTLE TANK

remote weapons system
(gun fired from inside tank)

The M1 Abrams is one of the most technically advanced tanks in the world. It's a heavy, well-armed and well-armored machine, and it is the main tank of the US Army and US Marine Corps. More than 10,000 of these tanks have been built. There are three versions: the original M1, the M1A1, and the M1A2. Each improves on the one before.

M1A1 Abrams

Length: 26 feet (8 m)

Width: 13 feet (4 m)

Weight: 63 tons (57 metric tons)

Engine: Gas turbine

Top Speed: 45 miles (72 km) per hour

Weapons: 120 mm gun/ three machine guns

Armor: Composite

Crew: 4

The 120 mm gun is controlled by a digital fire control system, which improves accuracy by taking into account wind speed, air pressure, and the shape of the shell being fired.

driver's controls

driver's position

machine gun

gas turbine engine

wheels that drive tracks

The ammunition store separates from the turret in case of a direct hit, protecting the crew from explosions.

tracks made from linked metal sections

The crew is protected in their compartment from nuclear, biological, and chemical attack.

Composite armor is made of layers of different materials, so it is tougher than solid steel.

27

TIMELINE

14th century
Simple weapons using gunpowder, such as the pot-de-fer, are invented.

1485
Leonardo da Vinci sketches a man-powered armored fighting vehicle.

12th century
The trebuchet, similar to the catapult, is developed in Europe.

1586
The Tsar cannon is made.

19th century
Explosive shells that explode on impact are developed.

1861-1865
Guns with rifled barrels are used widely during the American Civil War.

1914-1918
Artillery is used on a massive scale to attack enemy trenches during World War I

1917
British Mark IV tanks break through German lines at the Battle of Cambrai.

9th century CE
Gunpowder is invented in China.

1428
Simple cannons are used at the Siege of Orleans in France.

1784
Henry Shrapnel invents a shell that releases bullets, known as the Shrapnel shell.

1940
The first Russian T-34 tank is built.

c. 500 BCE
Armies of Greece and Rome are using weapons such as battering rams and giant crossbows.

1939-1945
Powerful tanks are used for high-speed attacks on the enemy during World War II.

1453
Wrought-iron cannons help in the siege of Constantinople.

1915
The first experimental tanks are built in Britain and are used in battle.

c. 2000 BCE
Warriors are going into battle in horse-drawn chariots.

1902
In England, Frederick Simms builds the Simms Motor War Car, an early armored car.

FACT
FILE

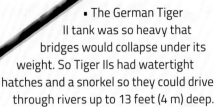

1942
The first German Tiger tank goes into action.

- The German Tiger II tank was so heavy that bridges would collapse under its weight. So Tiger IIs had watertight hatches and a snorkel so they could drive through rivers up to 13 feet (4 m) deep.

- World War II began with sweeping attacks by hundreds of German tanks, known as the panzer divisions. Nothing could stop them.

1998
The first British Challenger 2 tank goes into service.

- Today the word *shrapnel* means a piece of metal from a shell. The word comes from Henry Shrapnel, who invented an exploding shell.

1979
The M198 Howitzer goes into service.

- British guns fired nearly two million shells at the German line in a few days at the start of the Battle of the Somme in 1916.

1980
The first American M1 Abrams tank goes into service.

- The largest tank ever to go into mass production was the French Char 2C, which was 33 feet (10 m) long and weighed 76 tons (69 metric tons). It was used between 1921 and 1940.

- The heaviest tank ever built was the Panzerkampfwagen VIII Maus (the Mouse), weighing 207 tons (188 metric tons). Only one Mouse was completed.

- During World War I, the British built a giant explosives factory in Scotland. The explosives were dangerous to handle because they could easily explode, and the sloppy mixture of chemicals used to make them was known as Devil's Porridge.

GLOSSARY

A siege tower, often used to storm castle walls under siege

bore: the inner diameter of a gun's barrel

cannon: an artillery piece that uses gunpowder or other explosive material to launch a projectile

cannonball: a solid ball of iron or stone fired from a cannon

cast: to form a material into shape by melting it and pouring it into a mold

composite material: a material made from two or more other materials combined together

explosive: a substance that burns so fast it creates a shock wave in the air that destroys everything around it

field artillery: guns that move around the battlefield

gunpowder: a grey powder that burns fast and explodes, producing heat and gas

mortar: a short-range artillery piece

Panther: a German medium-sized tank of World War II

panzer: the German word for a tank

projectile: any object fired through the air

range: the distance from a gun to its target, or the maximum distance that the gun can fire

rifling: grooves on the inside of a gun's barrel that make a shell spin as it's fired

self-propelled artillery: a vehicle with a large gun but no armor

shell: a metal cylinder with a pointed end that is fired from a gun and which explodes on impact

shrapnel: a piece of metal shell case released when a shell explodes

Eighteenth-century cannonball

A muzzle loader artillery piece from the American Civil War

siege: a battle in which a defending army locks itself inside the walls of a city or castle, and an attacking army tries to break in

wrought iron: a pure form of iron, easy to shape but not stiff

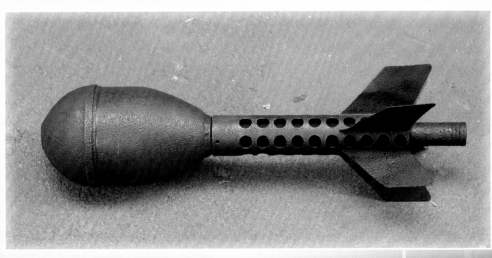

German mortar shell from World War II

INDEX

The Author

Chris Oxlade is an experienced author of educational books for children with more than two hundred titles to his name, including many on science and technology. He enjoys camping and adventurous outdoor sports, including rock climbing, hill running, kayaking, and sailing. He lives in England with his wife, children, and dogs.

Picture Credits (abbreviations: t = top; b = bottom; c = center; l = left; r = right)
© www.shutterstock.com:

3 c, 9 c, 11 bl, 13 tr, 14 br, 18 tl, 20 b, 21 tl, 28 tl, 28 bc, 29 tl, 29 bl, 30 br, 31 tc, 31 bc, 32 r.

FC, c = Cody Images. 2, l = 615 Collection/ Alamy Stock Photo. 4, c = Andrew Harker / Alamy Stock Photo. 6, b = Cody Images. 7, c = Cody Images. 8, all = Cody Images. 11, t = Niday Picture Library / Alamy Stock Photo. 12, tl = Cody Images. 12, b = © Boykov / Shutterstock.com. 14, cl = Andrew Bargery / Alamy Stock Photo. 15, t = Cody Images. 15, b = INTERFOTO / Alamy Stock Photo. 16, t = Chronicle / Alamy Stock Photo. 16, b = Military Images / Alamy Stock Photo. 17, b = Cody Images. 19, t = World History Archive / Alamy Stock Photo. 20, tl = Cody Images. 21, b = Cody Images. 22, cl = ITAR-TASS Photo Agency / Alamy Stock Photo. 22, b = Oliver Bunic / Bloomberg / Bloomberg via Getty Images. 22-23, c = PJF Military Collection /Alamy Stock Photo. 23, t = Cody Images. 24, cl = Cody Images. 24-25, c = andrew chittock / Alamy Stock Photo. 25, t = Cody Images. 29, cr = Everett Collection Historical / Alamy Stock Photo.